Bertha's Secret Battle

JOHN COLDWELL

Illustrated by Doffy Weir

OXFORD
UNIVERSITY PRESS

OXFORD
UNIVERSITY PRESS

Great Clarendon Street, Oxford OX2 6DP

Oxford University Press is a department of the University of Oxford.
It furthers the University's objective of excellence in research, scholarship,
and education by publishing worldwide in

Oxford   New York

Auckland   Cape Town   Dar es Salaam   Hong Kong   Karachi
Kuala Lumpur   Madrid   Melbourne   Mexico City   Nairobi
New Delhi   Shanghai   Taipei   Toronto

With offices in

Argentina   Austria   Brazil   Chile   Czech Republic   France   Greece
Guatemala   Hungary   Italy   Japan   Poland   Portugal   Singapore
South Korea   Switzerland   Thailand   Turkey   Ukraine   Vietnam

Oxford is a registered trade mark of Oxford University Press
in the UK and in certain other countries

British Library Cataloguing in Publication Data
Data available

ISBN: 978-0-19-917975-6

5 7 9 10 8 6

Available in packs
Stage 11 Pack of 6:
ISBN: 978-0-19-917973-2
Stage 11 Class Pack:
ISBN: 978-0-19-917980-0
Guided Reading Cards also available:
ISBN: 978-0-19-917982-4

Cover artwork by Doffy Weir
Photograph of John Coldwell © Caroline Scott Photography, Staplehurst

Printed in China by Imago

Twins

Bertha and Fiona were twin sisters. They looked exactly the same. There was only one way to tell them apart. Bertha dyed her hair red and Fiona dyed her hair blonde. The twins lived together in a cottage.

On Friday evenings they set off for work at the Town Hall.

A sign outside the Town Hall said, 'Grand Wrestling Competition.'

The referee stepped under the top rope and into the ring.

'Ladies and gentlemen. Silence please for tonight's star fight.'

The doors of the dressing room swung open.

'And here she is,' cried the referee. 'The darling of the ring. Fairplay Fiona!'

A cheer went up from the crowd.
Fiona, dressed in pink, came into the
hall. Her blonde hair streamed behind
her. With one leap she jumped over
the top rope and landed in the ring.

She waved to the crowd and blew
them kisses. The crowd stood and
clapped. They wanted Fiona to win.

The referee spoke again.

'And her opponent for tonight is...'

The dressing room doors smashed open. One door came of its hinges.

'Her terrible twin sister. Big Bertha the Bone Cruncher!'

Bertha, dressed in black, came into the hall. Her red hair streamed behind her. She took a flying leap into the ring. She shook her fist. The crowd booed. They wanted Bertha to lose.

The referee turned to check his watch.

Bertha grabbed Fiona and threw her against the ropes.

The crowd yelled at the referee.

Bertha raced back to her corner. The referee turned round.

'I haven't done anything wrong,' shouted Bertha.

The fight had begun.

Fiona bounced back with a flying drop kick.

The crowd stood up, cheering.

Bertha picked up Fiona and spun her above her head.

The crowd booed.

So it went for five rounds.

'And the winner is – Fairplay Fiona.'

The crowd cheered Fiona. They booed Bertha.

That night Bertha and Fiona sat at home drinking cocoa.

'I thought the fight went very well,' said Fiona.

'Hum,' said Bertha.

'You're not upset about the flying tail spin?'

'No.'

'The drop kick in round two?'

'No.'

'Then why are you in such a bad mood?'

Bertha began to cry.

'What's the matter?' asked Fiona.

'Well,' sobbed Bertha, 'people always cheer you and they always boo me.'

'That's because I am Fairplay Fiona and you are Big Bertha the Bone Cruncher,' said Fiona.

'Couldn't we change?' said Bertha. 'You could be "Fearsome Fiona". I could be "Big-Hearted Bertha".'

'Don't be silly,' said Fiona. 'Besides, you are good at being bad.'

'You could teach me how to be good,' said Bertha. 'And I could teach you how to be bad.'

'No!' said Fiona. 'What would my fans think?'

Bertha fights back

Next Friday morning, after breakfast, the twins went into the front room. They put the table and chairs in a pile at one end of the room. They moved the television, the goldfish bowl and their books into the kitchen.

When the room was completely clear, Fiona said, 'Ready?'

'Ready,' said Bertha.

Then the twins began to fight. Bertha threw Fiona across the room. Fiona did a perfect cartwheel and landed lightly on her feet.

The twins always practised for the fight on Friday night. Both twins were very skilled at wrestling. They worked hard to make sure they could do their moves without hurting each other.

When they had finished practising they had to tidy the cottage and have lunch. The twins liked cooking but they hated housework. They tossed a coin to see who should tidy up.

'Heads,' said Bertha.

'Tails,' said Fiona. 'I win.'

So Bertha had to move all the things from the kitchen back into the front room. Then she had to put the table and chairs back in the middle of the room. Meanwhile, Fiona cooked lunch.

After lunch Bertha slipped quietly
into the bathroom and locked the door.
Bertha rinsed her hair with her sister's
blonde hair colour. She looked in the
mirror and smiled. Her hair was now
blonde, just like Fiona's. She poured the
rest of the blonde hair colour down the
sink. Then she filled the bottle with
some of her red hair colour.

Fiona tapped on the door.

'Hurry up in there,' she called.

'Nearly finished,' replied Bertha.

'I must colour my hair before I go jogging,' said Fiona.

Bertha came out of the bathroom. She had a towel wrapped around her head.

'I feel much better,' said Bertha. 'I've left the bathroom tidy.'

'Look at the time,' said Fiona. 'I shall be late.'

Fiona dashed into the bathroom. She splashed on her hair colour. She was in such a hurry that she did not look in the mirror.

'Have a lovely run,' said Bertha.

Fiona jogged down the road.

She ran through the park. Fiona saw a little kitten sitting on a wall.

'Hello, little kitty.'

She stretched out to stroke the kitten. The kitten ran up a tree.

A policeman was passing by.

'I saw you frighten that kitten. What an unkind thing to do.'

'I only tried to stroke it,' mumbled Fiona.

She jogged on towards the playground. Some children were playing on the swings.

'Would you like a push?' she called.

The children took one look at Fiona. They jumped off the swings and ran away.

The park keeper raced up.

'What do you think you are doing? You were chasing those children. Go and chase someone your own size.'

Fiona ran off.

Fiona stopped for a rest outside
the supermarket. An old lady was
pushing her trolley towards the door.

Fiona ran over to help. She held
open the door.

'After you,' she said.

'It's a trick. You are going to shut the
door in my face,' said the old lady.

The manager arrived.

'Stop frightening my customers.
Clear off before I call the police.'

Fiona could not understand it. She
jogged sadly back to the cottage.

Bertha was in the garden.

'What have you done to your hair?'
cried Fiona.

'Do you like it?' asked Bertha.

'It's blonde. That's my hair colour,'
said Fiona.

'Is it really?' said Bertha. She took a mirror from her pocket. She held it up to Fiona.

'My hair!' screamed Fiona. 'It's red! But that's your colour.'

'I know,' said Bertha.

'Everybody will think that I am you,' said Fiona.

'That's right,' giggled Bertha.

'I will have to do my hair all over again,' said Fiona.

'You can't,' said Bertha.

'Why not?' asked Fiona.

'Because I tipped your hair colour down the sink,' said Bertha.

'But we are due at the Town Hall in ten minutes,' moaned Fiona. 'What are we going to do?'

Heads or tails?

The Town Hall was packed with people
waiting to see the big fight.

The referee stepped forward.

'Ladies and gentlemen. In the red
corner. Fairplay Fiona.'

Bertha, dressed in pink with her
blonde hair flying, raced forward and
jumped into the ring. She waved to the
crowd. Everybody cheered.

'And in the blue corner is that monster of the ring, Big Bertha the Bone Cruncher.'

Fiona, dressed in black with red hair streaming, crashed her way towards the ring. She shook her fist at Bertha.

The crowd thought that she was shaking her fist at them. They booed.

The fight began. Fiona and Bertha gripped each other by the shoulders.

'How do you like being the bad one?' hissed Bertha.

'It's horrible,' said Fiona. 'Everybody wants me to lose.'

'Now you know how I feel,' whispered Bertha. 'Right. I'm going to throw you over my shoulder.'

And that is just what she did. The crowd cheered. Bertha waved at the crowd and smiled.

'And the winner is Fairplay Fiona.'
Bertha, with blonde hair and dressed in
pink, waved. The crowd cheered.

The two sisters sat in the dressing
room as the crowd went home.

'I don't know why you're looking so
pleased with yourself,' said Fiona.

'Because I won,' said Bertha.

'But you didn't win,' said
Fiona. 'The referee said that the
winner was Fairplay Fiona.
And that's me.'

'Oh,' said Bertha.

There was a
knock on the door.

'Come in,' called Fiona.

A little man carrying an enormous
bunch of flowers slid shyly into the
dressing room.

'I've brought some flowers for Fiona,'
he said.

'How kind,' smiled Fiona.

The man walked past Fiona and
handed the flowers to Bertha.

'I'd just like to say,' he said, 'that you
are my favourite wrestler.'

Then he went very red and ran out
of the room.

'Hey,' said Fiona. 'He said those
flowers were for me.'

'Oh no,' said Bertha. 'He gave them
to me.'

'Really,' snapped Fiona. 'This is
absolutely ridiculous.'

'I've been thinking,' said Bertha. 'I
have an idea that should keep
everybody happy.'

'Let's hear it then,' said Fiona.

'Every Friday,' said Bertha, 'we toss a coin to see which one of us dyes their hair red and which one dyes their hair blonde.'

'No,' said Fiona. 'I can't agree to that.'

'In that case,' said Bertha, 'I shall keep my hair blonde. Then we can both be Fairplay Fiona. Nobody will come to watch two Fionas fighting. So we won't get paid. Then we will have to sell the cottage. Then...'

'All right, all right,' sighed Fiona. 'I agree.'

And so every Friday the two sisters clear the front room and practise their moves. Then they toss a coin to decide who has to do the housework. And after lunch they toss the coin again to decide their hair colour.

Sometimes it is Bertha with blonde hair and Fiona with red hair. Sometimes it is Fiona with blonde hair and Bertha with red hair. And nobody in the crowds that come to watch them fight has ever noticed.

About the author

I was born in London in 1950 and now live by the seaside, in Ramsgate. In the evening I like to write stories and poems. I do this very quietly. Then I go downstairs and play jazz records very loudly. My family think that I do two very daft things. One is going up the garden every night looking for frogs, newts and hedgehogs. The other is supporting Gillingham Football Club.